What Would I Look Like If I Were a Snoman?

Summary: Zack loves building snowmen and often wonders what he'd look like if he were a real snowman. After a long day outside, his wish is about to come true!

ISBN 978-1514303788

*To our son, Zack, who completed our family,
and kept us on our toes; to my husband, who
has loved me through good and bad.*

I know if my parents,
Howard and Millie Fisher, were still with us,
they would be proud.

Zack waited a long time for this day to come. Snow had fallen throughout the night. This snow was perfect. Deep and wet. Just right for making snowmen.

Zack got dressed and darted out the door.

4

While friends were having snowball fights and sledding down the big hill in town, Zack was busy making snowmen.

6

Each one was different. Some were tall and thin, some were short and round. They all had different hats and scarves. Some wore smiles made of coal. All of the snowmen had a bright orange carrot for a nose.

Zack was having so much fun creating all of his snow friends that when he looked around, the whole yard was full!

8

Zack's favorite snowman had eyes made of big blue buttons, a slightly curved carrot nose, and a big, floppy, brown hat. He was very tall and round, and stood as proud as a prince.

10

At the end of the day, Zack was tired and cold and went inside. His mom made him a bowl of chicken noodle soup to warm him up.

As Zack slurped his soup, a thought came to him. What would he look like as a snowman?

He thought about it some more while he took his bath and got ready for bed, and more than ever while his mom read his favorite snowman story, and kissed him goodnight.

He just could not get the thought of what he would look like as a snowman out of his head.

The next morning, his mom was busy getting him ready for school. But, wait! She was not getting his jeans and sweatshirt out of his dresser.

No, she pulled a carrot out of the fridge, grabbed a big, floppy, brown hat, and got her sewing kit to find buttons. What was she doing?

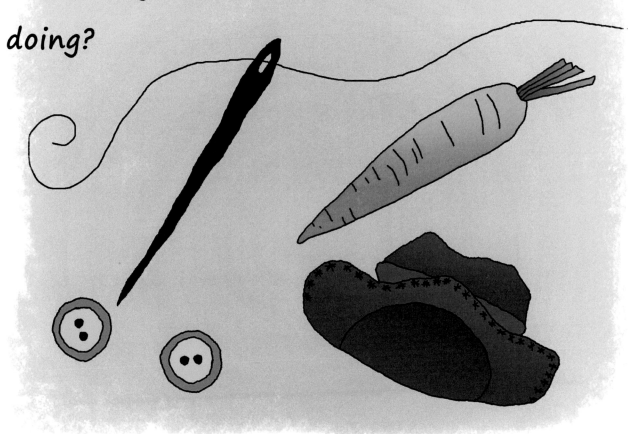

She stuck the cold carrot right in the middle of his face, where his nose should be. Above that, she put the green buttons on, just where his eyes used to be. Then she put his favorite brown, floppy hat on his head.

18

She gave him his lunch and a kiss, then sent him toward the door. Zack was so very confused. How could he go to school like this? Had his mom lost it? Zack slowly walked to the door, and as he passed a mirror in the hallway, he could not believe his eyes.

Could that really be? It was him: he was a snowman! Zack slowly smiled and said, "So this is what I would look like as a snowman!"

With a smile on his face, he rolled over, and woke up to another snowy day.

Acknowledgments

Thank you to my cousin, Angela Townsend, who showed me that anything is possible. Thank you for spending so much of your time making my dream a reality, but most of all, thank you for bringing my words alive with your drawings.

A special thank you to Toni Kerr, Mariah McGarvey, and Jeri Miller, who helped me up the many steps on the stairway to publication.

About the Author

Renee Fisher-Martino was born and raised in Spokane, Washington. Due to her love of children, Renee pursued a degree in early childhood education, and has taught preschool for 33 years.

The idea for this book came from writing a lesson plan for snowmen: one of the activities was "What would I look like as a snowman?" and the ideas for this book came flooding in. Renee lives in central Indiana with her son, Zachary, and her husband, Michael.

About the Illustrator

Best-selling author, Angela J. Townsend was born in the beautiful Rocky Mountains of Missoula, Montana. As a child, Angela grew up listening to the ancient tales and legends of faraway places, told by her grandparents. Influenced by her Irish and Scottish heritage, Angela became an avid research historian, specializing Celtic mythology.

Her gift for storytelling and history finally came full-circle as a published author. Angela's love of regional lore, mythology, and history, brings a unique perspective and compelling voice to her novels.

Angela's novel, Amarok, published by Spencer Hill Press in 2012, made the Amazon best seller list in three separate categories. She is also published by Clean Teen Publishing and Crimson Tree.

Angela's other published works, including River of Bones, Angus MacBain and the Island of Sleeping Kings, Angus MacBain and the Agate Eyeglass, and Moonflower, have all been well received. The novel, The Forlorned, is scheduled for release in July of 2015. The movie based on her novel, and directed by Andrew Wiest, is due out in 2015.

angelatownsendbooks.com

Interior Design

Toni Kerr is a DIY full time artist whether she wants to be or not. She writes young adult novels, takes on illustration and design projects, and restores historic murals when such times arise. She enjoys building tree houses, not-so-fancy chicken coops, and tends to forget how much maintenance is required for certain types of landscape designs.

She lives with her husband, two dangerously creative children, an Australian Shepherd, and several small farm animals the city would probably frown upon.

artistryforauthors.blogspot.com

25281731R00020

Made in the USA
San Bernardino, CA
24 October 2015